MW01463138

Pioneer Families

Thelma Rea

The Rosen Publishing Group's
READING ROOM
Collection: Social Studies™
New York

Published in 2006 by The Rosen Publishing Group, Inc.
29 East 21st Street, New York, NY 10010

Copyright © 2006 by The Rosen Publishing Group, Inc.

All rights reserved. No part of this book may be reproduced in any form without permission in writing from the publisher, except by a reviewer.

Book Design: Ronald A. Churley

Photo Credits: Cover, pp. 1, 4, 6, 8, 10, 12 © Corbis-Bettmann.

ISBN: 1-4042-3346-6

Library of Congress Cataloging-in-Publication Data

Rea, Thelma, 1971-
Pioneer families / Thelma Rea.
p. cm. -- (The reading room collection. Social studies) Includes index.
ISBN 1-4042-3346-6 (library binding)
1. Pioneers--West (U.S.)--History--Juvenile literature. 2. Pioneers--West (U.S.)--Social life and customs--Juvenile literature. 3. Frontier and pioneer life--West (U.S.)--Juvenile literature. 4. Log cabins--West (U.S.)--History--Juvenile literature. 5. West (U.S.)--Social life and customs--Juvenile literature. I. Title. II. Rosen Publishing Group's reading room collection. Social studies.
F596.R369 2006
978--dc22
2005011892

Manufactured in the United States of America

Contents

Time to Go	5
The Trip West	7
Log Cabin Homes	9
Living in a Log Cabin	11
Work to Be Done	13
Helping Each Other	14
Glossary	15
Index	16

4

Time to Go

In 1760, many **colonists** who lived on the East Coast of the United States decided to move to the western part of the United States. The **pioneers**, who were the first group to **settle** in the West, wanted their own **farmland**.

Pioneer families traveled hundreds of miles to find new land. They brought tools, clothes, and food in their covered wagons.

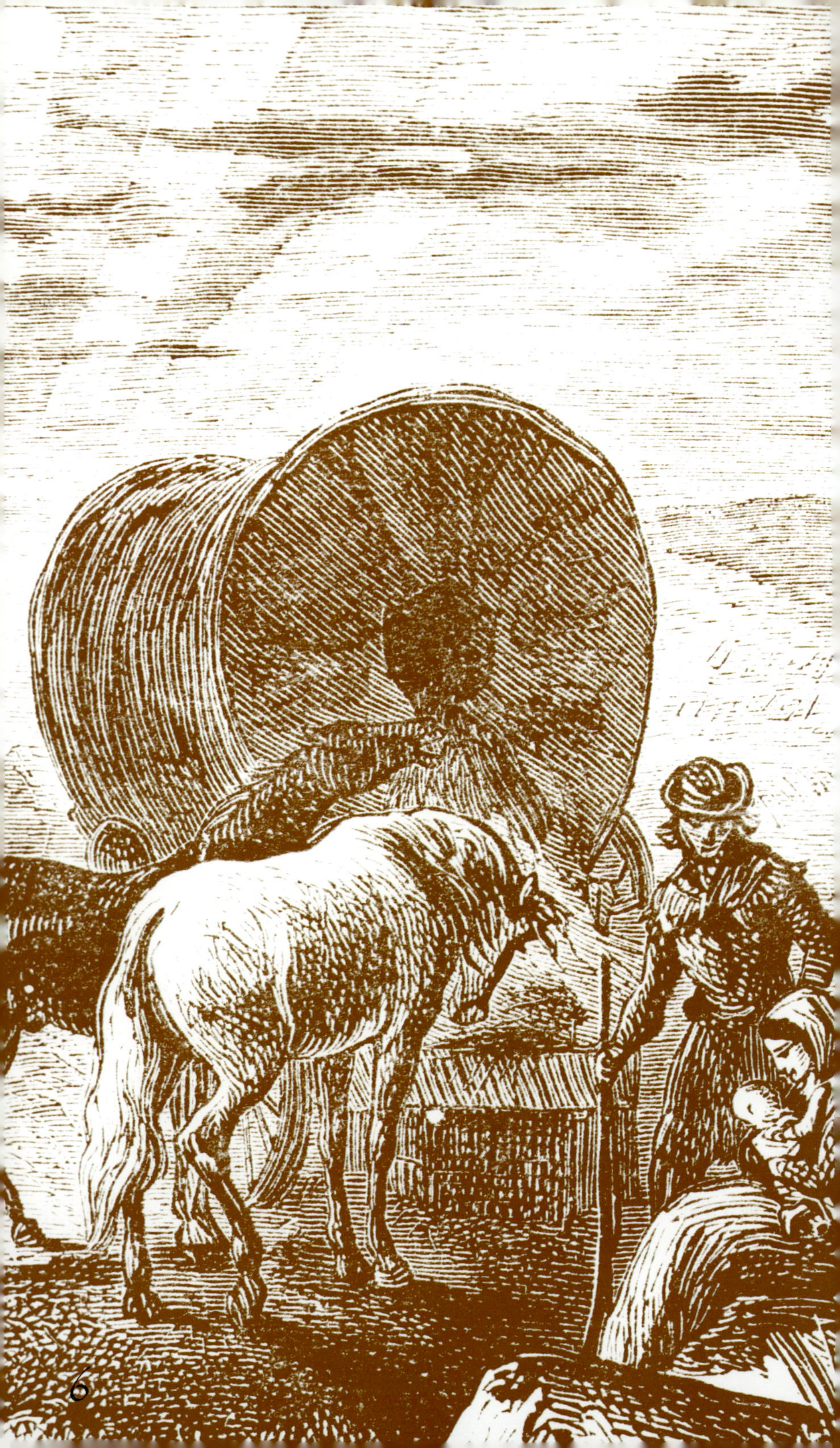

The Trip West

Pioneer families traveled in covered wagons for many days. Groups of pioneers traveled together in **wagon trains**. Once families found some land they liked, they cut down trees and planted **crops**. Later, they made logs from the trees to build their homes.

Pioneers camped out while they planted crops and built their homes.

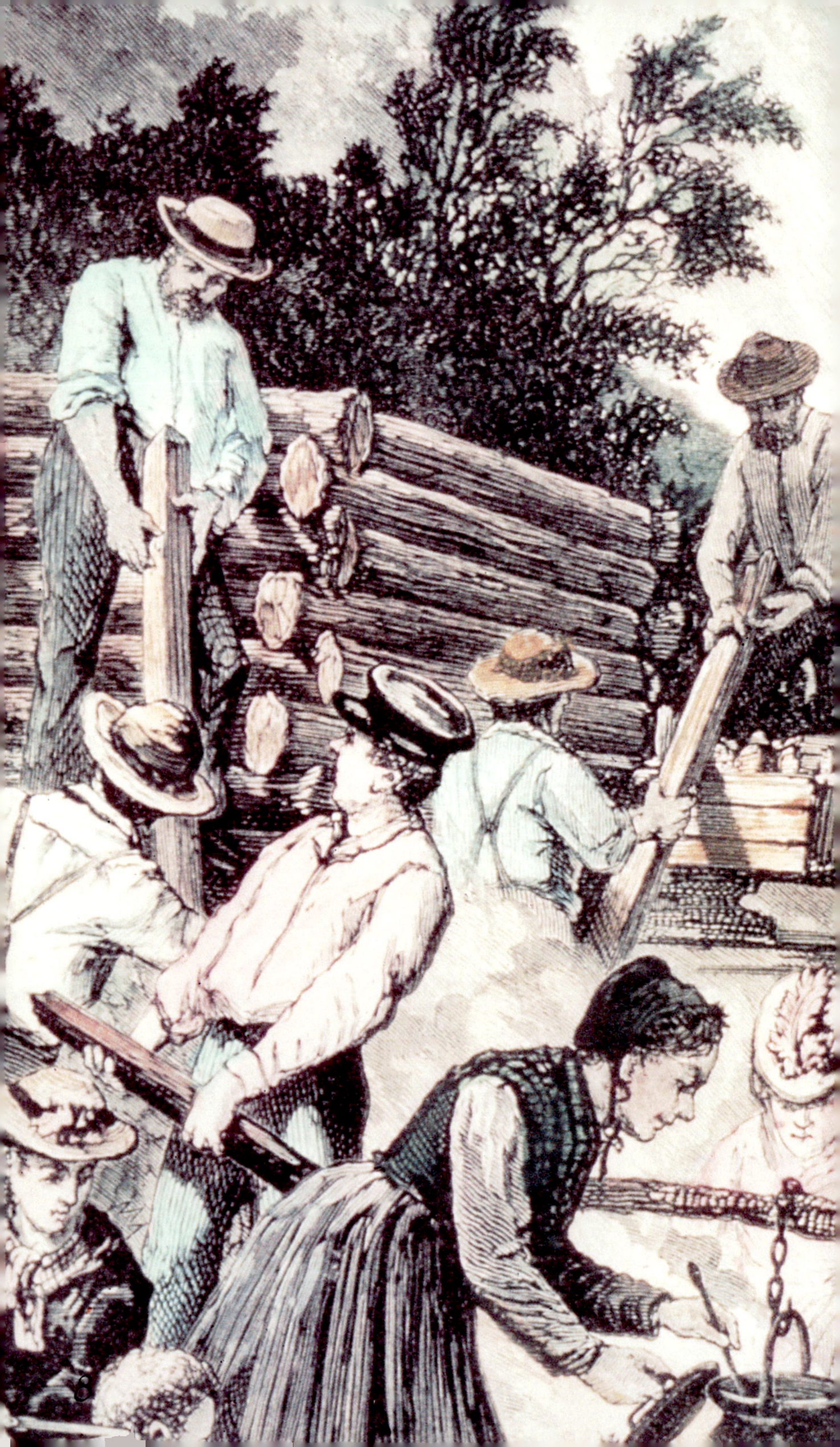

Log Cabin Homes

Everyone worked together to build each home. Pioneers cut **notches** at the ends of the logs so they would fit together. Then they filled the spaces between the logs with clay, moss, and mud. This helped keep the homes warm and dry.

Pioneers built log cabin homes from the trees they had cut down.

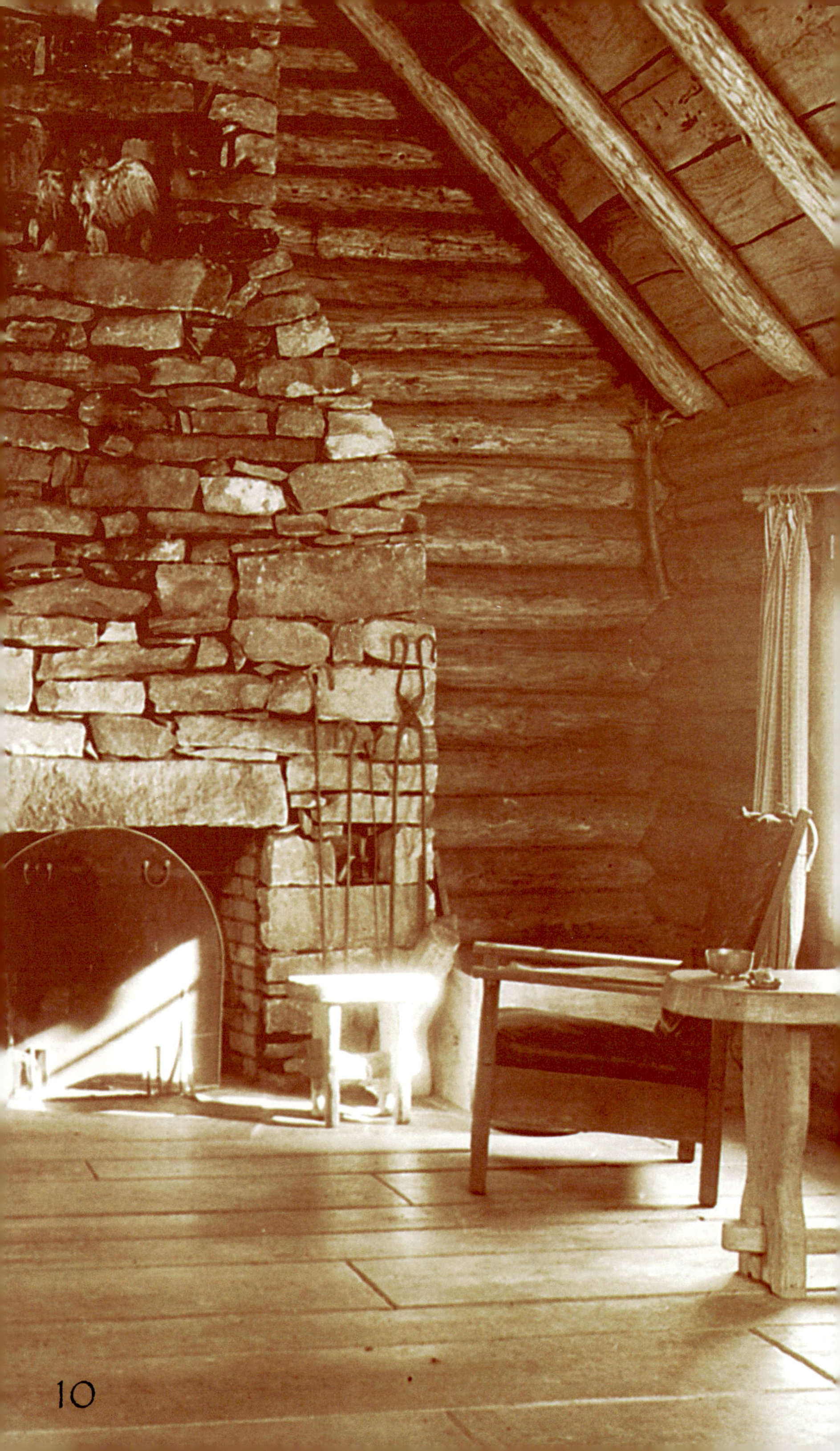

Living in a Log Cabin

Inside the log cabin, pioneers made fires in a fireplace to cook and keep the house warm. Mothers cooked simple meals of vegetables and meat in a big pot. Fathers made tables and chairs for the kitchen from logs.

Many people still like to live in log cabin homes and use handmade wooden tables and chairs.

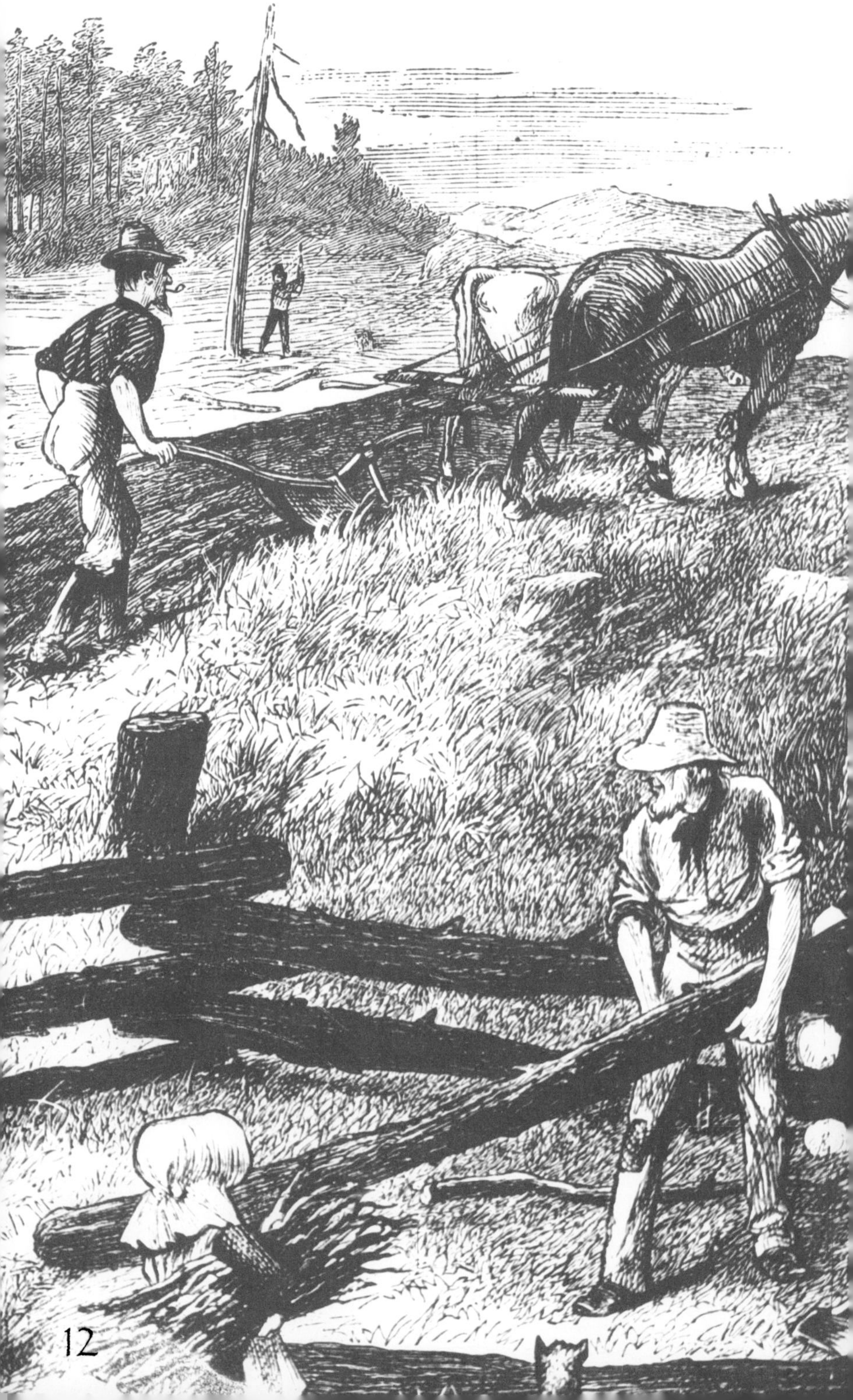

Work to Be Done

Pioneer children worked hard in their new homes. They gathered eggs from the chickens and milked the cows. Children also fed the farm animals and brought in wood for the fire every day.

Every person in a pioneer family had an important job to do.

Helping Each Other

The pioneers **depended** on each other. If someone was sick or needed food, everyone helped out. They helped each other plant seeds and build homes. Pioneers started a new life in the West with the help of their friends and neighbors.

Glossary

colonist — A person who lives in one country but is under the rule of another country.

crops — Plants grown by farmers for food.

depend — To need someone and know that they will help you.

farmland — A piece of land on which someone grows his or her own food and raises animals.

notch — A V-shaped cut made on the end of a log.

pioneer — A person who settles in an area where very few people have lived before.

settle — To live in a new place.

wagon train — A group of people traveling together in a line of covered wagons.

Index

B
build, 7, 9, 14

C
cabin, 11
colonists, 5
crops, 7

F
farmland, 5
fireplace, 11

H
homes, 7, 9, 13, 14

L
log(s), 7, 9, 11

N
notches, 9

P
pioneer(s), 5, 7, 9, 11, 13, 14

S
settle, 5

W
wagons, 7
wagon trains, 7
warm, 9, 11
worked, 9, 13